Spinning away, the assassin raced for the western wall, bounding swiftly up the steps to the ramparts. Turning, he sent a look out across the estate, and could see that the first guard had already reached the corpses. Another roar rose up into the night sky, and away towards the main gate, the first alarm bell began to ring out across the grounds.

Also by Anthony Lavisher

The Storm Trilogy

Whispers of a Storm
Shadows of a Storm
Vengeance of a Storm

The Last Tiger

With Jamie Wallis

Vengeance

Anthony Lavisher

Solstice

of a

Storm

A Chronicle of the Four Vales

Dear Myfanwy

Here's to adventure, and
wherever it takes us !

7.10.21

This one's for you.

Acknowledgements

A few years ago, following the conclusion of the Storm Trilogy, I could never have imagined that my adventures would take me back to the Four Vales so soon.

Destiny, it appeared, had other plans for me, and following the chance of a publishing deal that, sadly, would not come to fruition, I was left with a new version of Whispers of a Storm, and a beautiful map of the Four Vales.

The novella you are about to read was always planned to be released by my publisher, and I am pleased, finally, to be able to share another tale, perhaps the first of several returns, to the land that many a reader has enjoyed exploring with me.

Before we set forth together again, I would like to, once more, thank Omercan Cirit for his fantastic cover art and Charlotte Rees for her invaluable care and attention.

And finally, but by no means least, I would like to thank all of you who have kept me going these last few years with your unerring support and kindness.

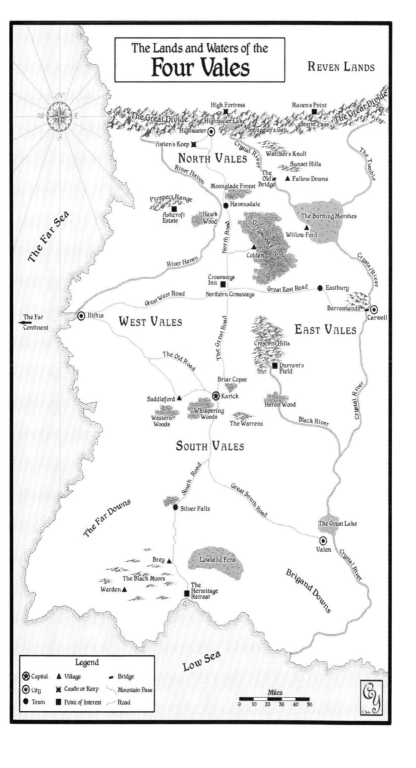

CHAPTER ONE

Cobwebs

It was night by the time the Keeper of the Dead pulled close the rickety door to his drafted hut, and sat near to the meagre fire to warm his hands over the flames. Urging the rusty kettle to boil, he glanced to where it hung from a hook above the hearth, impatiently waiting to retrieve it and make himself another pot of lavender tea.

Casting a fretful look to the single, cracked window of the hut, he flicked his tongue nervously across the back of his teeth. That damned impenetrable fog was still there! It wouldn't go away. Last year it had lasted for nigh on a week, and here it was again, billowing like a ghost at his window and blanking out the world outside.

The fog haunting the woods had lasted for almost two weeks now. It was a residual spectre that enshrouded the land and outlying farmsteads to the south of the city of Karick in its silent embrace. Sapping at the morale of the people who gloomily went about their daily lives in a state of caution, it forced them to fix one eye on their work, the other worriedly to the sounds that whispered to their imaginations through the unwelcome opaque curtain.

Historically, gloom was not all too unfamiliar for the inhabitants that lived and worked the lands to the south of the capital of the Four Vales – for many seasons the woods and Great Road to the south of Karick had been ruled by marauding outlaws and brigands; travellers and merchants attacked and waylaid for little more than the cloak off their backs. As the robberies began to turn more sinister, and the increasing reports to the Valian authorities were heard daily from the bereaved, the presiding ruler of the Valian Council, the High Duke, Karian Stromn, had sent a sizeable force into the woods to the south-west of the capital – commonly known as the Bandit Woods – to root out and put a stop to the nefarious activities operating from there, once and for all.

During a cold, bitter winter, the High Duke's men hunted down the brigands, killing them where they hid, chasing them through the South Vales for weeks and finally to their new refuge in the Far Downs, hanging all who were captured in the decisive battle that followed.

As the memory of darker days faded, and the seasons slipped away, peace returned to the region, and the Bandit Woods, formally a dark place of foreboding and fear, was renamed the *Whispering Woods*, in honour of the dead that would one day come to be buried there when the city's graveyards and catacombs were full.

What have I done? The Keeper wondered. He had asked himself that very question for several weeks now, since his fortunes had changed – not for the better – and as always, any answer was not forthcoming. Since that fateful day, and for fear of her safety, he had spent many nights away from his wife, staring deep into the solace of his empty cup of *Burning Leaf*, seeking the solution to his dilemma within the dancing flames of his fireplace.

The Keeper shook his head ruefully as he began to fold up the dirty cloth in his shaking hands so that he would not burn his skin on the kettle presently. For six winters now, he had tended to the graveyard on the eastern borders of the Whispering Woods, since the previous tenant had joined the ranks of his charges. His father had been found dead beside the grave he had been digging for yet another imminent occupant; his heart finally giving up after several years of illness.

It was then, somewhere between a mixed-sense of duty tainted by loss, that his son had taken up the offered mantle, inadvertently inheriting his father's nickname from the inhabitants of the city. The Keeper of the Dead.

He hadn't paid much heed to the good-natured banter that came his way, and had carried on his father's work with pride. Lovingly tending to the grounds, weeding, cutting the lawns and perimeter hedgerows that offered some solitude to visiting mourners to the graveyard, already abundant with graves beyond its capacity, he cared for the headstones, keeping them free of moss and removing the flowers brought by loved ones, once they had withered. Every day he would visit his mother and father's graves and talk to them, telling them he was to be a father himself soon, and that he hoped, one day, to give them a grandson to carry on his father's name and work.

Full of hope and merriment at being a father, he had been thinking a lot of that day recently, sometime in the next few months, when he would hold his child in his arms and give him, or her, a welcoming name to the world.

And then his prospects had changed...

It had been mid-evening, several weeks ago now, as he was weeding the graves of his parents, when he was approached by *them*. Coming from the city, they arrived at dusk, bringing with them their promises of a better life, their offer of coin, silently weighted down by unsaid threats. With apparent little choice, other than to lose his life, the Keeper had reluctantly agreed to their proposal, unwilling to allow them to carry out their parting threats that '*They wouldn't want anything to happen to his unborn child.*'

It would only prove to be the start of his problems. If the Keeper's decision to help them, for fear of keeping his family safe was bad enough, things would get even more complicated two weeks later, when he was approached in the city, as he headed down the Valian Mile.

The Keeper's thoughts snapped back to the present as the water in the kettle began to hiss and bubble over with impatience, spitting its distaste onto the flames below.

Staring at the cold, angry bruise of warning on his left wrist, the Keeper shuddered and snatched his focus back to the kettle. The chill that crawled up his spine needed curbing and, wrapping the cloth about his hand, he reached for the only warmth that he would feel that night.

As his shaking hand stretched forth, an unnatural sound split the cold night asunder and he jumped back, the cloth unfurling from his limp grasp as it fell unnoticed to the dusty floor.

Voices floated through the night, barely audible, but clearly noticeable in a place where only the dead resided. The Keeper stumbled to the window and wiped away the condensation building up on the broken pane. Pressing his nose to the glass, he stared out into the dark, blinded by the fog and choked to breathlessness by his fear. He had known this day would finally come, but he had secretly prayed that it would not...

"I can't see a damned thing out here!" muttered the tall, lean figure dressed in dark leathers and a tattered cape, as he stumbled into an unseen headstone and cracked his knee. Swearing, he bent low to furiously rub away his pain and cast a derisive look towards his shorter, older companion.

"This 'ad better be worth it," he complained bitterly, "coming all the way from Ilithia. Surely we could have got something closer to home... where it's not so bloody foggy?"

His companion shook his head in exasperation, wishing that his usual partner, his friend Garret, had not got caught by the Watch three weeks ago, whilst robbing a tomb in Ilithia – the capital of the West Vales.

With time running out, and the demands from his employer growing ever louder and more dangerous in his ear, in desperation, he had been forced to turn to Garret's eldest son, Tal. He sighed, looking for the lad in question. Waiting for the *boy* to catch him up, he pretended not to notice the mortal limp he had suddenly acquired.

"Just as well we did!" the older man muttered to himself. Realising that he had spoken aloud, he coughed in embarrassment. "If you can't negotiate a bit of fog—"

"A *bit* of fog?" the wounded youth observed incredulously.

The older man shrugged, grinning inwardly. "If you can't handle a bit of fog on your first job, what in the Storms would you do in the city, blundering about in the shadows, trying to avoid the Watch? Eh?"

His apprentice fell silent and glanced about his surroundings in embarrassment.

"I'll tell you how you would have done. You, no *we*, would now be dangling from a Valian rope. I agreed to show you the ropes because your pa is still waiting to call in his favour, true enough – but it will be a different kind of rope if you don't shut up."

Although his tone was still soft, the ferocity in the old man's eyes shamed the younger man deeper into his silence.

"This is why I brought you along on this job – this foggy wood – out of sight of all we need to fear. It's easier to rob graves when there are no guards waiting to stretch your neck."

"S-sorry boss," Tal mumbled, chastened. He was clearly afraid, his nerves breaking across his face like a cold wave.

Smiling gruffly, his mentor passed him a large crowbar from the pack he carried and motioned him through the fog towards the west side of the graveyard.

"Come on lad," he urged him, his breath clouding. "This will be the easiest job you ever do, it's all arranged. All we have to do is break into his tomb and give the grave keeper his cut on our way out. With luck, we can be back on the road to Ilithia before sunrise."

Tal gripped the crowbar and nodded, following as his master moved by him. As he picked his way through the maze of headstones, he cast a quick look back towards the tiny hut, hiding in the fog and under the shadows of a large elm, in the north-east corner of the graveyard.

He wasn't sure, but it looked like someone was watching them. Tal just hoped it was the man who had been *persuaded* to let them come here.

The Keeper watched the pair as they bickered their way across towards the west side of the cemetery, where two large crypts awaited them. They were so cock-sure they would not be caught – everything had been arranged and they knew it. The Keeper felt sick and tore his gaze away, hiding under the window with his back against the wall.

Please, Lady, let it be over quickly…

"Which one is the old man buried in?" Tal asked quietly, as they stood facing the two mausoleums. Several bats swooped into view, and then wheeled away again into the dense soup-like fog as they hunted for their supper.

"He's supposedly in the larger of the two," replied his mentor. He could hear the fear in the young man's voice now, but chose to ignore it.

The night felt like it was closing in upon them. The moon was a blur behind the dark clouds, and the graveyard harboured the unnerving chatter of the unknown.

Nearby, an owl hooted, causing Tal to start with fright. Placing a calming hand on the lad's shoulder, his mentor guided him forward to the impressive tomb on their left. A pair of lions reared up on either side of the stone entrance, snarling in permanent salute.

"Looks like the Keeper's saved us some time, Tal!"

The young man had also noticed that the stone doorway had already been hauled open for them, and feeling the warming promise of success, they moved to the shadowed entrance. Creepers and vines hung from the opening, and a spider busied itself with the rebuilding of its web in one corner.

"How'd he know we were coming tonight then, boss?" Tal wondered, wrinkling his nose at the musty smell of dust and dead air that emanated from within.

"The agents acting on our employer's behalf within the city told me that the Keeper would open the nobleman's tomb every night for two weeks, just before midnight, so that we could come and go unhindered."

Tal was not convinced. "If it was going to be this easy,

why were we hired to do the dirty deed? If he had agents in the city, why send us all the way out here?"

A fair question.

"Because he's a coward, a rich, powerful coward," came the reply. "You had best not think about who's paying us, just be thankful that we are getting paid. If we all *shut up* and get on with this, we will be set up for a couple of years – just like the grave keeper. This way, he can also have a better life, and not get killed. He lets us in, closes up once we are gone, and nobody's the wiser. It's quite a good idea actually! Shame that the Keeper of the cemetery in Ilithia isn't quite so unscrupulous."

As Tal continued to jump at every little sound, the older man fished within his pack and pulled forth a pair of flax-tipped torches. "Hold these, lad."

Tal took the torches and held them up, as his mentor produced a tinder and flint from his pack.

A swift strike later, and the resulting sparks flamed both torches to life. Tal passed one back to his master, and he accepted it carefully, avoiding the hot tallow dripping from the burning flax.

"Let's get this done."

They moved cautiously to the entrance, and the eerie light spilled into the darkness beyond to reveal a narrow flight of dusted stone steps that fell away into the unknown beneath them.

"Must have been richer than I was told," the older man mused, scratching at his beard with his free hand. "I half-expected to find the sarcophagus above ground, not below in a burial chamber."

Tal didn't care, he just wanted to get this over with and get out of the graveyard. It felt like a thousand eyes were constantly watching him, but there was nobody here to witness his first crime except the headstones jutting above the carpet of fog, the bats, and that bloody owl.

As if on cue, a huge white owl drifted lazily into view and glided silently across the graveyard, its large yellow eyes searching keenly for a rodent to dine on. Tal marvelled at the hunter's grace, wishing he could move just as silently on foot, and was then dragged roughly inside the tomb.

The torches cackled and spat as they descended into the darkness below, smoking tendrils of flame licking hungrily at the veils of cobwebs as they burnt their way into the dust-choked chamber below.

Their shadows sprang to life on the walls of the burial room as the light spilled out into the area before them. In the centre of the chamber, a large, ornately carved sarcophagus drew their immediate attention. A thick layer of dust covered the heavy stone lid and a cold brazier rested on its surface. In the darkness beyond, they could just make out the shadowy form of a large chest, cloaked heavily in cobwebs and dust.

Tal swallowed, licking his lips nervously. He was finding it hard to breath in the dense, dead underground air, and he wasn't sure if he could stay down there much longer – no matter how excited he was at the prospect of his first haul!

"Right, let's get this lid off." The old man's voice sounded distant as he placed his torch in an empty bracket on the wall behind them. Tal dropped his onto the floor, where it sputtered in a cloud of dust motes.

Positioning themselves on either side of the sarcophagus, they faced each other silently for a time and then the older man smiled.

"Right, to me. Ready?"

Tal nodded, his eyes fixed on his master's. In the

flickering shadows, he did not notice that the dust on his side of the sarcophagus had already been disturbed. As one, they both heaved on the heavy stone lid.

For a time nothing happened, except for the burning of muscles and the corners of stone cutting into straining, sweating palms. And then, just as Tal thought his shoulder blades would explode from their exertions, the stone lid groaned with protest and slid slightly free. The trapped air inside sucked in a fresh breath and spat out a geyser of dust, showering the younger man who immediately fell back, spluttering and coughing.

Deren Aaron watched his young apprentice, chuckling. "Now you know why I said '*to me*' youngster. Remember this trick – I did, after my mentor played it on me the first time I robbed a tomb."

Tal was too busy wiping the dust from his mouth and eyes to care as Aaron pulled the lid further free, and then moved round to pick up the fallen torch. Even the experienced grave robber's heart was pounding at the anticipation of the treasure within. This was to be his finest moment, his crowning achievement. The money he received from the recovery of the nobleman's sword within would allow him to finally retire.

Flames glowed in his bright, gleaming eyes as Deren Aaron shone the torch inside.

"I don't understand," Tal said at his side, peering into the sarcophagus. "There's nothing here! Just a withered old corpse! Where's the sword then? Where's the rest of the loot?"

Deren Aaron frowned, reaching in to turn the body over. It began to crumble at his touch.

"I'm not sure lad. It should be here! He would have been buried with it," he paused glancing over at the heavy chest. "Perhaps it's in there."

Tal began moving over to it, and then froze. Deren turned, looking back to the staircase. They had both heard a sound, and it felt as if someone was there with them.

Ssh! Aaron whipped his hand to his lips, as Tal was about to speak. He placed the torch on the lid of the half-opened sarcophagus and slid forth a long-bladed knife from the sheath at his waist. Stepping away, he motioned for Tal to follow his lead, and the lad, his eyes wide with fright, drew his Valian long sword from its scabbard. As one, they padded to either side of the torch lit archway and peered up the stairway.

At the top of the stairs, barely visible in the weak moonlight, and aglow in the fog's luminance, they could see a dark figure. It was cloaked and hooded in shadows, motionless, as it stood there watching them both, one shoulder leaning against the old stone.

Tal flicked a glance at his master, his lips trembling. "W-what do we do?" he whispered.

The figure at the top of the stairs regarded them both silently, arms folded across its chest, and they faced each other wordlessly for several heartbeats.

Suddenly, the cloaked figure pushed itself away from the wall and began to amble down the stairs. Tal shrank away as the stranger's footfalls echoed on the stone. Outside, the owl hooted once again in what could almost be described as anticipation.

"Who are you? Stand fast, or I'll gut you this night," Deren growled, as the hooded figure continued its descent. "Stay back, or by the Storms the Keeper will have another corpse to bury."

At this the stranger stopped, cocking its hooded head to one side as if considering his threat and then carried on.

"Couldn't have put that better myself," the hooded

11

figure said, laughing.

It was a man's voice, and as Tal looked to his master, the hooded figure leapt down the remaining stairs towards them, his gloveless hands flashing into view, each wielding a short, slender blade.

Their attacker, cloaked all in black, leapt into the burial chamber in a trail of shadows, easily turning aside Tal's clumsy lunge. Shouldering him aside, the man spun past Deren Aaron's murderous cut, intended to gut, and hammered the older man across the back of the head with the hilt of his right blade.

Tal winced as he heard the dull crunch of bone, and watched helplessly as his master crumpled, his blade clattering from his limp hand across the stone floor.

The hooded attacker turned then, his swords, twin swords, hanging loosely at his sides.

"So here's the choice," the man said, his piercing grey eyes flashing in the torchlight. "You can die with your sword in your hand, or my swords in your back. What'll it be?"

Tal felt his legs weaken and grimaced, fighting to keep a hold of his bowels. He flicked a look to his father's best friend, before sending a furtive glance towards the stone steps and his freedom.

The man shook his hooded head, dragging Tal's attention back with a chiding tut.

"What do you want from us?" Tal squeaked, somehow finding his voice. "There was no treasure, anyway. Just let us go, please – we won't tell a soul."

Two steps through the dust before the lad could react, the man's left blade had opened up the youth's throat, and as he stepped past, he left his other blade deep in the tomb robber's back.

"I know you won't," the swordsman hissed, watching on dispassionately as the young man dropped his steel and clutched vainly at the life spilling through his fingers.

Tal dropped to his knees, coughing up his last few breaths, blood pumping into the stale air before him. As his vision began to fade, as he dropped to his knees and pitched forward into a cold blackness, the last thing he would see in this life was the hooded attacker stalking forward to drag his master towards the tomb.

"Wake up!"

The slap to his face roused Deren Aaron from his unconsciousness, and for a time his head pounded out an angry tune, his surroundings swirling about him. When his vision finally snapped back into focus, the tomb robber found that he was resting with his back against the carved, hard stone. Groaning, he tried to grasp hold of what had happened, why he was there, and when he finally did, his lolling eyes found Tal's still form – face down in the dust, his life pooling about him, glistening in the flickering shadows.

"That's on you," the hooded man pointed out, from where he leant against the side of the open sarcophagus. He had his arms folded against his chest, and Deren could see that he wore a black leather jerkin and that his forearms were protected by dark, studded leather bracers.

Deren groaned, shifting his body to turn and look at the hooded figure. He couldn't see the man's face as it was hidden below the eyes by a dark scarf – but he could see the eyes, those piercing eyes full of disdain, smouldering with controlled anger.

"I have all night," the man announced. Coming closer, he knelt beside the tomb robber, who held his gaze defiantly. "We can do this the hard way, or the easy way.

You choose."

Deren Aaron swallowed his fear, his mind racing. Whoever had sent this man here, had known they were coming... had their employer sent them here to die? Had he failed him somehow?

Unsure of what to say, Deren shrugged.

Shaking his hooded head, the swordsman drummed the fingers of one hand across the lid of the sarcophagus, playing out a silent tune in the dust.

"The treasure was never yours," the man stated. "Just like the other treasures you have been stealing to demand around the Vales – yes, I know, *we* know what you have been up to – what we can't figure out however, is who has been hiring you."

Deren Aaron felt his bowels begin to loosen from the fear spreading through his numb body. *How did they know? Who were they?*

"You didn't think the families of those you have robbed would let you get away with it, did you?" the man mocked, folding his arms across his chest again. "You really are the worst of us, you know that? I am a ruthless bastard, too, I know it. But the dead deserve their rest. Where is your honour man?"

The tomb robber remained silent, but his head dropped slightly.

The swordsman dragged one of his twin blades free and forced the older man's head up with the tip of his blade.

"Last chance for some dignity, Deren," the man stated, ignoring the shocked look the tomb robber dealt him. "Tell me who hired you! You owe them nothing – you are *nothing* to them."

Deren Aaron licked his dry lips and closed his eyes. Sighing, he puffed out his cheeks and shook his head.

"I may be many things, but I'm not a rat," he hissed.

His tormentor cocked his head to one side, nodding. "And neither would I be." He knelt on one knee beside the older man, leaving his sword at his throat as a pointed reminder. "Come on man! I am not one to give chances, but I am tired. I have spent nearly two weeks freezing my balls off each night, waiting for you fools to turn up. Tell me who sent you and I'll let you go. On my word, you can walk away from this."

Noticing the strange crescent-shaped knife sheathed at his waist, Deren Aaron looked up into the man's eyes, seeing the torchlight burning there. He shivered. This man was a killer, he wouldn't hesitate to pin his throat to the sarcophagus... but he also knew he meant what he said.

The tomb robber flicked a glance towards his best friend's son. Closing his eyes, he drew in a deep breath, held it there for as long as he could, drinking in his last, before letting it out again in a remorseful cloud.

If he squealed, he would live – but his family would all die... it would be better this way.

"Do your worst," Deren Aaron growled, spitting his defiance into his captor's masked face.

CHAPTER TWO

Shadows

Screams echoed through the night, rolling across the graveyard to drown out on the high hedgerows on the east side of the cemetery. The Keeper started from his spot under the window and began to sob uncontrollably.

For a time, there was silence, and then a higher, almost feminine scream rose up and was cut short.

The Keeper buried his head in his hands and wept. *What have I done? What have I become?*

He rocked back and forth, his mind tumbling in a maelstrom of unwanted questions and accusatory answers. *I had no choice! What choice did I have?*

He couldn't put the events of the past few weeks into words, or even conjure a sane, rational confession to ease his conscience. But he knew that from now on, unlike his charges, he would not find any peace.

Desperate to protect his wife and unborn child, he had readily agreed to the offers forced upon him – had accepted the promise of coin to help his conscience cope with what he was doing. But now, after this night, after the lives that had been lost, could he ever rest well again?

Sighing, the Keeper looked to the worm-riddled table, daring to look at the artefacts, wrapped tightly in the old, fraying cloth. He had guarded the sword and jewels for some days now, since the hooded man's first visit to him – since the stranger had '*robbed the tomb, to save the tomb*', as he had put it.

The Keeper shuddered. The mysterious man, who had approached him on the Valian Mile with his employer's counter-offer, went about his business with a calm, cold ruthlessness that left the Keeper certain that he had chosen to betray the right people. If he had refused the hooded man's advances, he knew he would no longer be alive.

For what seemed an eternity, long after the screams had ended, the Keeper remained under the window, his knees drawn up to his chin, his arms wrapped tightly about his shaking frame. In truth, it was no more than an hour, but finally, when his body was stiff with cramp, he dragged himself up from his hiding place and dared to look out the window.

The moon was radiant now, the fog subsiding. Dark shadows played tricks on his tattered mind, and the Keeper jumped at every sound he imagined coming his way. Wiping away his misting breath from the glass, he dared to look at the tomb.

It was shrouded in darkness – no torchlight shone from within, no sounds could be heard.

Letting out a thankful breath, the Keeper sighed, turning away towards the stove and the desire for a calming cup of tea. It was then that he heard the door handle turn.

"What do you want?" the Keeper sobbed. Staggering

back, he stumbled into the table, scattering its contents across the dusty floor as a hooded figure swept into the hut.

"Hold on there, Keeper," the man said, holding up empty hands. "I just want some warmth, before I leave you in peace."

Fumbling over the words he could not find, the Keeper waved a shaking hand towards the hearth, as he bent low to gather up the fallen artefacts.

"You can return them to the tomb, now," the stranger said, without looking back. As he held his hands over the flames to warm them, the Keeper could see that they were covered in blood.

"P-please, don't hurt me," the Keeper begged. He went to rise again, but his legs would not work. "I did all you asked of me – I won't tell a soul, you have my word."

The hooded head turned his way. "I know you won't," the man said, returning his attention to the fire.

By the time the Keeper's legs and arms worked again, and he had finished gathering up the treasures taken from the tomb some twelve days before, the hooded man had warmed himself enough to rise again.

His eyes glittered in the poor light as he spoke. "Your payment will arrive tomorrow," the man said, turning for the door. "Remember your word, Haysten Fenn. You do not want to see me again."

"Wait!" the Keeper called out. "What about *them*? What do I do with the bodies?"

"Do what you do best," the man said, his voice rich with amusement. He opened the door and stepped out into the night, a shadow once more.

*

It was quiet in the sewers that night, and after another long night in the cold, the hooded man was glad of it. It wasn't always so, however, and even though he could come and go as much as he pleased without fear, he knew that there was always some fool, desperate or otherwise, waiting to prey on those that preferred the labyrinthine tunnels beneath the city of Karick, to its choked, bustling streets above.

The man shook his head. To him, there wasn't much difference. There was just as much shit clogging the streets above as there was below. At least down here, the stench was an honest one. Of late, the peace and so-called prosperity that the Four Vales had been enduring for several decades now was starting to crumble; although most of the idiots who paid their taxes with a smile and a thank you to the collector, had not yet realised it.

In the High Duke's marbled halls, the political divide, clearly there, but relatively peaceful for some time, was starting to show. Divisions were widening, deepening cracks were beginning to develop between the old guard, the hardliners on the Valian Council, and the reformers. The former, those that if they had been around fifty years before would have wanted the Valian Armies to march back across the mountains to the north and finish off the Reven tribes that had been threatening the Four Vales, once and for all – the latter, those that had spared the Reven people, not taking the chance to seize their mineral-rich lands, whilst their tribes were scattered and broken, all those years ago.

The current High Duke, Karian Stromn, was also a latter; a man of peace, who ruled fairly and justly in his father's memory, and as far as the hooded man could tell, was well-loved by the people.

The man laughed. When the peace eventually broke,

and the man knew that one day soon it would – he would make an absolute fortune from the fallout, he could sense it.

Carrying on his way, the moving shadow slipped unnoticed through the sewers. Fortunately, of late, there had not been too much rain, and the ancient, crumbling pathways were clear of sewerage and deep pools full of anything you wouldn't want to walk through.

As he stepped into another low tunnel, several rats scurried away from the light of his waning torch, and the man knew he had better reach his destination soon, lest he run out of light.

Hurrying on his way, the hooded wayfarer passed by a pathway, leading away into the darkness towards the north, and he slowed to a distracted stop. He felt his skin prick in cold remembrance as a vision of darker days plagued his memory. Scowling, the man could feel the pain, even now, in the pit of his back and, cursing, he scattered aside his past and plunged, with even more determination, towards his future and the wealth that was waiting for him.

He finally reached the blank wall as his torch began to cough and sputter in protest, and placing it in the empty bracket, fixed to the wall on his left, he hammered an impatient fist upon the faceless stone before him.

Nothing! He hammered again.

By the time his hand was aching and he was ready to kick the blank wall down, he heard the distant sounds of footfall, and finding a breath he reined in his fraying composure. He was tired, he knew that, and he would need a clear head for the negotiations that were to follow. He had the upper hand now, and he needed to focus his thoughts.

When the wall slid silently to one side and a lantern's light spilled down the corridor, the hooded man failed to hide his disappointment that it wasn't the woman who met him this time.

"You took your damnedest time," he snapped.

The hideous apparition before him was squat and ugly, his arms covered by tattoos of the kind of women he could only ever dream of getting his fat paws upon, and he studied the newcomer with his one good eye.

Dressed in clothes that were covered in grease, grime and worse, the red-haired man's face flushed in the light. The ugly brute sucked in a deep, calming breath between his rosy cheeks before he replied.

"The boss wanted to see you, as soon as you returned," the short man said. He was trying to hide his anger, the man could tell. "Follow me."

"I know the way," the hooded man replied moving forward, but the door-keeper stood his ground.

"I'm Cullen," the squat man said, thrusting a hairy arm and hand into the space between them.

"Good for you," came the reply, followed by a brief, unwanted handshake.

Swallowing further words, the lantern bearer allowed his guest entrance, closing the secret door behind him. Dragging in a deep breath, Cullen stared up the steep set of narrow stairs before them and led the hooded man up slowly into the small chamber above.

Passing through the room, which had only four chairs gathered about an old table, the shorter man led the newcomer on. After a time traversing along several nondescript stone passageways, Cullen led the man up a short set of steps and into a richly carpeted corridor. Paintings lined the wall, and the hooded man, once again, felt that he was in some nobleman's house, not the sewers.

Licking his dry lips beneath his scarf, the man felt his

pulse quicken. He was about to come into some serious coin again. It had been a few months since his last job and his habit of whores and opiates was draining his resources.

Halting at a dark, wooden door, Cullen knocked upon it. He waited for a moment before opening it up to move inside the room beyond. Muffled voices were heard, and then the ugly man was back, jabbing his head towards the room.

"You can go in," Cullen announced. He stepped aside as the hooded man swept by him without thanks.

Muttering, the squat man pulled the door shut and headed back along the corridor.

He's trouble, that one, Cullen thought.

"It gladdens me to see you," the man sat behind the huge antique writing desk greeted, as the door closed behind his guest.

Flicking a quick look about the room's opulence, the hooded man headed over to the chair that was offered to him by the seated man. The room was furnished like a study, wreathed in candlelight and surrounded by shelves full of books and parchments, and as the lean man rose and offered him his hand, the hooded man's attention was drawn to the painting of a wolf, howling away to a bright moon, on the wall behind his employer's head.

"Well met," the man said, as they both sat down and faced each other across the ink pot and parchments on the desk. "You have news, I take it, Arillion?"

The hooded man eyed the man before him. He was into his thirtieth summer, perhaps more, but his eyes, those dark eyes, were slanted at the corners, revealing his heritage – a mix of Valian and Reven – making him look far too young for the forked, neatly-trimmed beard he sported.

The man was a wealthy merchant and dressed in the finest robes to prove it, having risen to some prominence over the last few years, despite the prejudices he faced both above and below the city. He leant forward as his guest remained silent, folding his hands patiently before him.

"Were you successful?" the merchant-thief asked.

Arillion lowered his hood and pulled his face mask down, revealing the handsome, strong face behind the shadows. "I was," he nodded, smiling.

He could see the merchant's face light up and whilst he had the advantage, Arillion pressed on. "It took nearly two weeks, but your people did their work well. The fools were after the old man's treasures, as you suspected, and they sent two other fools to rob the tomb."

The merchant, Savinn Kassaar, clasped his hands tightly together. As he leant even closer across the desk, Arillion could see the whites of his knuckles.

"Did you find out?" Savinn dared to ask. Arillion knew the merchant had a lot riding on this, and he could see the desire burning away in his eyes.

Arillion sat back in his chair, ignoring the press of his blades in his back. He nodded. "From the moment we shook hands, you were going to find out. You hired me for this very reason."

Savinn nodded his head, calming his eagerness with a deep breath and smile of acknowledgement. "It has taken me several years to gain your attention, Arillion. I hope my patience, and my coin, was worth the effort?"

Arillion chuckled. "More than you could have ever known. Before they died, I found out that the name of the man who hired them, though it was not who you thought – it was Edward Merrick."

Savinn blinked, leaning back into the arms of his shock.

23

He had made many enemies in the last few years, particularly those on the Valian Council who despised his swift rise to both wealth, and political prominence. There were many foes, he knew, but he had not thought to count the unassuming Merrick among them.

"I can see you are confused," Arillion stated. "I would have wagered, if I was a gambling man, that it would have been one of the bastards that blocked you from the table."

Savinn arched an eyebrow in surprise. Arillion's reputation, though by deed and not by name, was well known. It was said on the street, that if you wanted something done, the mysterious swordsman, the assassin, was the man you needed to find. It had taken Savinn many years to finally find him, and he had wasted much coin on various ventures that had failed to come to fruition in the meantime because of the people he was forced to hire – but he could tell, now that he had the chance of revenge, Arillion was the perfect tool to sharpen his wrath upon.

The hardliners, chiefly the Lord of the East Vales, Henry Carwell, had blocked his nomination to join the Valian Council the previous summer, when Lord Farrington, the Lord of the South Vales had died suddenly. Keen for an appointment that they could control, Lord Carwell and his supporters had piled their coin, power and support towards the nomination of Lord Farrington's only son – despite the fact that the High Duke and his allies supported Savinn's own campaign.

Losing by five votes to three, Savinn's thirst for even greater political prominence, and the High Duke's own hopes for a more balanced Council table, had been thwarted.

It had stung the merchant-thief, deeper than he cared to admit, and Lady Rothley, the old, dangerous, and bitter steward of the West Vales, had not been one to shy away from showing her double-edged disgust.

'*My commiserations for your loss,*' she had penned him. '*I share in your disappointment, but I bask in this victory for Valian reason and sense.*'

Savinn scowled. Even now, that letter cut deeply, and he wished that he had not burned it...

"So what are you going to do?" Arillion asked, bringing the merchant back to the table.

The merchant licked his lips thoughtfully. "Edward Merrick has political aspirations, beyond his capability. I know it, he knows it, and the people know it. It is a great risk he is taking, but this need for such treasures might suggest that he is trying to fill his coffers for the bribes he will undoubtedly have to offer in the future."

"Maybe," Arillion sounded bored, and he picked at the stitching of his cloak. "That's for you to decide. I am only interested in what you want me to do about him, if anything?"

Savinn sat back again and regarded the man, the assassin, sat across from him. He licked the worry from his lips, banishing the thought that he would not want anyone to send this dangerous man after him, was thankful that the last attempt on his life had failed.

"Hmm," the merchant-thief mused, stroking his bearded chin. "Most of the Council, their staff, their hangers-on, are making their way to Highwater at the moment for the Solstice Games that will take place in two weeks' time. Merrick will be there, I am sure, currying favour, hanging off the shoulders of those he would garner support from. Perhaps... hmm, just perhaps..."

Arillion had already figured that part out, but was happy for the merchant to come up with the idea himself. It was obvious that Merrick, an insignificant merchant, would be there, it was the perfect opportunity to be rid of him – what was surprising though was that Savinn did not seem in a hurry to make his own way to Highwater, the capital of the North Vales.

Arillion rose, clapping his hands together to keep them warm. "Well, when you think up a use for my services, you know where to find me."

He turned, making his way to the door. His left hand touched the handle, before the merchant called after him.

"My thanks, Arillion," Savinn said, and actually sounded like he meant it. "I will have your money delivered to the broker, Kaylin Baric, as you requested."

Arillion turned as he pulled his scarf back up over his face. He nodded his thanks, pulling his hood up over his head. "One last thing! What happened to the girl who approached me, the one who tracked me down? She has a rare talent, that one."

Savinn smiled. "She has other tasks to perform for me these days. I have put Dia's skills and ears to better use."

Arillion shrugged aside his disappointment. "I'll wait to hear from you then, merchant."

Pulling open the door, the swordsman left the merchant-thief to his dilemma. Slipping from the hideout and sewers before the first light of the new day had touched the horizon, Arillion went to find the whores that would keep him company for the next few days, whilst Savinn Kassaar decided on how much coin he was willing to pay him for his next task.

CHAPTER THREE

Highwater

Kalen Rynn stamped his feet to sting the cold from his numb toes and blew hard on his gloved hands as he tried to keep them warm. The night had been a long one, especially as he was missing out on the last few nights of the Solstice celebrations taking part in the city below, and he still had another five hours before his watch was relieved for another day. Wrapping his cloak tightly about his frame, he moved closer to the torch, burning from a wall bracket on the west wing's entrance porch of the estate of the Lord of Highwater, Alion Byron.

It had been a long week of celebrations, and the city's streets, always bustling, were bursting with song, trade, merriment and, sadly, moments of violence. Kalen sighed. The summer had been a hot one in the capital of the North Vales, and as the high slopes turned to burnt-orange, and the leaves of the trees began to turn, the nights became as cold and crisp as the approaching winter.

Wishing he had not pulled the short straw in the barracks, that he had not been one of the many guards unable to join in the celebrations this season, Kalen could console himself that at least he had been picked to guard the Byron Estate, not sent down into the city to control the merriment and chaos.

He had been relieved when he had been hand-picked by his captain to be seconded to the Lord of Highwater's estate for the duration of the celebrations, to help guard the numerous dignitaries that had been personally invited to stay at Byron Keep. In two days, there would be a grand party held in the Great Hall of the Keep, and Kalen knew that it would be then that the hard work would really start.

The son of a modest livery stable owner in the city, Kalen had been enticed by his friend to join the ranks of the city's militia, five years ago, and his father, devastated that his son had turned his back on the family's business in order to fulfil some misguided declaration of independence, had barely spoken to him since.

Kalen whistled a tune quietly, willing his comrade's return so that he could have his turn at stretching his legs with a perimeter patrol. It was quiet in the keep at the moment as most of the household and their guests were down in the city, enjoying the celebrations and a play that recounted the greatest moment in Valian history, some fifty summers ago now, the moment that the Valian armies had defeated the Reven hordes gathering together north of the Great Divide, the vast mountain range that separated the Four Vales from the tribal lands.

The sky was cloudless, the dark night's canvas filled only with the brightness of a magnificent Solstice Moon – a fortuitous sign from the Lady of the Vales for the coming harvest season, the benevolent deity that many across the country were now starting to worship. Even though he was not one for the new religions, Kalen still offered up his thanks to the blessed Lady, for sparing him duties in the city below and, more importantly, for sending him Cassy.

Kalen smiled broadly, forgetting about the cold evening for a moment.

He had been out enjoying a celebratory drink in the *Celestial Raven* with those picked to guard Alion Byron's estate during the celebrations, when he had got talking to a lovely beauty. The young woman couldn't get enough of him, and over the next few weeks he had spent all of his spare time and coin to lavish gifts upon her.

He soon discovered that she had moved to Highwater from an outlying farm to the south, several months before, and was trying to find a job on a rich merchant's estate, where she would have better prospects and a safe roof over her head. Cassy had met with little success so far, and got by working the tables at several of the local drinking houses in the poor quarter of the city.

Kalen was besotted. She was the first and last thing on his mind. When he closed his eyes he could see her beautiful face and picture her dazzling smile. When they were together, it was as if nothing else mattered, and when they were apart, it was as if there was nothing else to look forward to but her return. She wanted to know everything about him – his family, his friends, and his past. He obliged her readily, and one night, when they were lying in bed together, Kalen had promised to help her realise her dreams. Whilst his duties kept him at the estate, he would try and speak to the head of the household, Elisabeth Bay, and get her a job at Byron Keep.

Cassy was elated, and in her excitement, she wanted to know everything about the estate. Once her lover started his work there, he told her everything he had seen and heard, each morning after his shift, when they could be together again, and she thanked him in the way that only she could.

Kalen's thoughts snapped back to the present with a grin, and he blew out a cloudy puff of excited breath. He was waiting for the right moment to ask the woman in charge of the house's kitchens if she could find a place for Cassy on her staff. She had been terribly busy with the preparations for the forthcoming banquet, but he would ask her once his shift finished – she would probably be thankful for the help. Kalen had not seen his lady for two days now, and it felt as if they had been apart for ever. He spoke about her constantly to his friends, and he was driving them mad with his love-struck ramblings. But Kalen didn't care, he was in love.

Heavy footfalls sounded on the path, and Kalen looked to the right to see a figure stumbling through the darkness towards him. In the moon's light, Kalen could just pick out the familiar cloak and armour of his friend, Thomas, on watch with him that evening.

Moving from the porch, Kalen raced to his friend's aid, as the younger man stumbled to his knees.

"What's the matter, Tom?" he asked. Kneeling beside his comrade, he searched for the face within the shadows of the bowed, hooded head. "What happened? Where is your torch?"

A dull pain exploded in Kalen's left armpit, and for a moment he couldn't decide what had happened, as confused images flashed through his head. He suddenly became aware of the strange warmth spreading through his body as his friend now began to support him. As he was laid upon the shale path, Kalen stared up at the grey eyes that looked down at him, glittering from within the shadowy hood. The guard blinked in confusion, his vision fading rapidly as a firm hand was clamped over his mouth.

"Shh!" a distant voice comforted him, as the question on Kalen's lips suffocated on his dying breath.

Arillion wiped his crescent-shaped blade on his victim's cloak, before dragging the body and fallen sword under a nearby hedgerow, away from the light of the porch. Checking the night for sounds of discovery, the assassin was pleased to detect nothing other than the revelry, echoing from the streets beneath the keep.

For two days now, since his arrival in the northernmost city of the Four Vales, nestled on the lower slopes of the Great Divide, Arillion had enjoyed the hospitality his newfound wealth was affording him. As promised, Savinn Kassaar had deposited his money with the broker, Kaylin Baric, a man Arillion trusted and had dealt with for many years. It had taken two days for the merchant-thief to contact him again, and by then Arillion had spent far too much coin on the pleasures and opiates he could not recall.

The creature, Cullen, had found him in a brothel, bearing a message and offer that Arillion could not, even if he had wanted to, refuse. Buoyed by the prospect of a greater sum of coin, the assassin had dismissed Savinn's messenger with his acceptance and assurances, before gathering his wits and striking out for the North Vales.

It had taken several days to reach Highwater, travelling the Great Road northwards through the central Vales, and then the North Road through the higher, quieter landscape that was the North Vales. By the time the towering peaks of the Great Divide slipped into view, Arillion shared the road with many other travellers, all heading to the city for the Solstice celebrations.

Slipping across the plains, away from the sprawling city

of tents and wagons that was amassing outside the capital of the North Vales, Arillion made his way east for several miles towards the narrow path that would take him up into the mountains and allow him to enter the city from the north; Smugglers Gap.

Aptly-named, for many years the narrow path had been used by those not wishing discovery by the Valian authorities; thieves, racketeers, smugglers, bastards. It was well known to those who chose anonymity, preferred to avoid scrutiny, or taxes, and Arillion knew the area better than most.

Despite the celebrations, already underway, Arillion slipped into Highwater from the north with little challenge from the guards there. Anyone coming down from the heights into the city was most likely coming from the fortress, anyhow. The High Fortress was the greatest bastion of Valian warning, built forty-five winters ago in the pass that offered the Reven the easiest route over the Great Divide into the Four Vales – it was a tall, grim, imposing fortress that warned the broken tribes not to repeat the mistakes of their forefathers.

As he slipped underneath the imposing gatehouse, Arillion was happy to let the guards think that he had come from the fortress, keen to be away from the frontier and take part in the fun. Joining in with the celebrations, Arillion had quickly found lodgings at *The Nest*, one of the better brothels established in the city, run by one of his old contacts, the beautiful, but ruthless, Morgan Belle.

Flame-haired, and with a temperament to match, the tall, fulsome woman had readily accepted her old acquaintance's money, quickly finding him a room when none were to be had and, two days later, the information he was seeking – the location of where Edward Merrick was staying. In Highwater, if Morgan Belle didn't know the information you were looking for, nobody would. Her girls and boys shared the beds of many notable figures within the city, and the steady line of information, that filled her coffers well, was always worth the coin and time spent.

Morgan had one of her girls, right now, deep in the confidence, ear and bed of several of the guards at Byron Keep. It hadn't taken the girl long, or much persuasion, to find out which dignitaries were staying at the keep and where they were housed.

Arillion's crowns had been well-spent, and despite the danger he would place himself in, the rewards waiting for him on Savinn Kassaar's table far outweighed the risks he would be taking. Although, as he paid his farewells and debts to the buxom brothel owner, Arillion was still not certain why Merrick, an insignificant figure at best, would have been personally invited to stay at Lord Byron's Keep.

Checking again for danger, the assassin stepped off the noisy path and made his way silently back around the grounds to the western side of the tall keep. He had spotted a balcony there earlier that would suffice, as he surveyed the guards and grounds from the shadows of the curtain wall. As he slipped through the moonlit night across the well-tended lawns, Arillion was pleased that his climb would not be interrupted now.

He smiled, though reined in his confidence. *This was proving too easy, so far.* Thanks to Morgan Belle's information, he had easily poisoned the six dogs kennelled at the rear of the estate, tossing joints of meat into their pens from the safety of the top of the wall.

Three of the guards patrolling the western wall of the Byron Estate had also been easily dispatched; such was the hour and their complacency, keen for their beds, wearily oblivious to the threat lurking in the dark. A swift change into one of their clothes and armour had allowed Arillion to draw the guard off his post at the front of the building. All he had to do now was gain access to the keep, find his mark's room on the second floor of the west wing, and wait for his prey to return from the celebrations.

Easy! Arillion frowned, the cold night biting the nape of his neck in warning. When the house returned, questions would be asked about the missing guards, and Arillion hoped that they would think they had made off to join in the celebrations, that a more detailed look into their absence would wait until a more hospitable hour. New guards would be stationed by the time he was done, and Arillion knew he would have to be careful in his escape.

He had not been to Highwater for several years, had not been able to – but that did not mean he did not keep up with news from around the Four Vales. Alion Byron was a fair man, it was still said. He was a man who protected the North Vales with the rule of law, but, unlike his counter-part in the East Vales, the ruthless Lord Carwell, Alion Byron was a respected man, loved by the general populace for his generosity and benevolence. A stalwart supporter of the High Duke, and therefore an enemy of the hardliners, he was a vociferous champion of peace and prosperity in the Four Vales.

So why in the storms would Edward Merrick be staying at the Keep? Merrick was a supporter of the hardliners, courting their favour with controversial speeches in the capital, hoping to garner their support. As insignificant a turd as he was, he had to shout all the more loudly – his words and hatred for those not of Valian blood, all the more distasteful.

Edward Merrick wanted to be everything that Alion Byron was not.

He didn't know the man, but Arillion respected the Lord of Highwater, and that was something he couldn't say about many people. Alion Byron's wife had died in childbirth and, bereft at the loss, the Lord of Highwater had not remarried, bringing up his daughter alone. Barely blooded, it was said that his daughter was a brat, running amok in the household, causing trouble where it could be found.

Arillion grinned, imagining the chaos and the headaches she would be causing her father. No stuffy nobility to be found there, just pure, selfish chaos. He liked the girl, already.

In the sparse moonlight, the assassin could see the dark balcony, blanketed in shadows and silence, as he looked up at the recently erected trellis that would allow plants to decorate the side of the building's wall in the summers to follow.

The assassin rubbed his bare hands together, blowing into his cupped palms. It was cold now, colder than it had been in the south, but Arillion preferred the colder north – it kept you focussed, it sharpened your wits.

Deciding to stay dressed in the dead guard's clothes, Arillion stepped into the flowerbed and tested the strength of the framework nailed to the wall. It would easily support his weight, as he had thought, the wood having not yet had the chance to be weakened and warped by the ravages of the weather and time.

With a final, wary glance about his surroundings, Arillion made his way silently up the trellis and dropped onto the balcony above. All was quiet, the celebrating city still oblivious to his presence.

Padding to the large double windows that acted as a door to the veranda, he peered through a break in the curtains and strained to see into the darkened bedroom beyond. Nothing! He could see nothing at all, and his breath misted up the glass as he planned his next course of action.

A slow test of the handles forced him to roll out a wallet of finely crafted tools and he perused along the line of moon-lit implements, finally selecting a thin hooked rod that he slid deftly into the lock. As expected, there was a key already there, and he withdrew a small cutting device that he rested against the glass and spun slowly round upon its spindle. The diamond-tipped blade easily cut through the glass and the sap-gummed pad in the centre of the device allowed him to quietly withdraw the circular piece of glass. If he had actually bought these tools, Arillion knew it would have cost him a King's ransom in crowns.

Replacing his tools, he pocketed the wallet within the folds of his cloak and left the piece of glass on top of the balcony wall. Flexing his numbing fingers, he slipped his left hand through the hole in the double windows and unlocked them from the inside.

The dull click made him wince as he opened the window and withdrew his arm. Listening for sounds of a disturbance within, Arillion was satisfied there were none. Slowly parting the heavy curtains, he stepped into the bedroom beyond.

The dark room inside was empty, his eyes tracing two large double sofas, facing one another across a low table. Lustrous carpets helped him quickly cross the lavishly furnished room to the door across from him.

The keep was still cloaked in silence, and the assassin pressed his ear against the cold wood of the door. Again, he heard nothing. It was as if the entire household was down in the city, but Arillion knew this would not be the case.

Alion Byron was not a man to rest, to allow himself the luxuries many others around the council table enjoyed. It was said that he spent all his time maintaining his seat at the table of power, supporting the High Duke when many others were being lured elsewhere. He was a man for his people, first and foremost, and should the hardliners ever have their way, have their war with the Reven, it would be the north that suffered the most from their ambitions.

Arillion licked his lips at the prospect. The growing divide was as brittle as poorly forged steel. The North and South Vales still had an alliance at the Council table; the East and West Vales opposing them constantly, growing stronger with each season. Firmly in the middle of this political anvil was the capital city, Karick, its ruler and people unaware of the hammer raised over their heads and the telling blow that would one day rain down upon them.

But that would be for another day. Usually, it was reported, Alion Byron would be up long into the early hours of the morning, locked away within the solitude of his study at the rear of the keep, pouring over the numerous accounts, planning his strategies to further the prosperity of the North Vales.

Arillion had been advised that there would normally be a dozen guards on duty at this time of the night, but tonight, as the household was down in the city with their retinues, there was probably only half that number, at best. Smiling to himself, the assassin quietly eased the door open and squinted as the lantern light from the hallway beyond dazzled his eyes. When he had adjusted to the brightness, he peered swiftly out.

A carpeted hallway swept to his left and right, decorated at precise points by gilt-framed paintings depicting portraits and landscapes. Three closed doors lined the wall adjacent to his position and there were two further doors on his side of the hallway. To the left, at the end of the hall, a large door stood closed and was fronted by a single guard, sleeping fitfully on a stool. To his right, he could see the top of a staircase that fell away to the ground floor below, and the other guards that would be patrolling there.

Slipping his crescent blade from its sheath, Arillion moved cat-quick to the top of the stairs and risked a glance below.

A lamp lit the stairs from a bracket on the wall, revealing a portrait of the Lord of Highwater, dressed in armour and looking imposing, as he welcomed those guests who looked upon the fine piece of art. The parabola staircase turned from his view into the silence below.

Contented, Arillion turned and swept down the hallway, away from the sleeping guard. Morgan Belle's girl had checked and thrice-checked the details of where Merrick was roomed, and Arillion already had a good idea in his mind of the room he was looking for. The keep was silent, not even the guard snored, and as he left the man to his dreams, Arillion slipped unnoticed through the night, past several doors, until he found the room he was looking for, two corridors away, the one with a painting of a black stallion hanging from the facing wall.

Arillion had stolen horses growing up, and he was fond of them. Taking the time to show his appreciation for the fine painting, the small nameplate underneath told him the beast's name was *Storm* – a fitting name for the thunder the stallion would make when it charged.

The room was locked, and Arillion withdrew his tools again, fixing a nervous eye on the hallway; lit by a single lamp, the light was poor, but he quickly had the lock open. Letting out a calming breath to steady his heart, the assassin could tell he was nervous. He was taking a great risk, for great rewards, yes, but it would be a lot harder getting out, than it was getting in.

With no window in the hallway, Arillion slipped quietly into the dark room beyond. Closing the door behind him, he pressed his back to the wood, drinking in the darkness, listening for sounds of danger. There were none. The small room was wreathed in shadow, elegantly furnished, but without a window. Arillion frowned. He had hoped for a swifter means of escape, but found comfort in the fact that even though he had been invited to stay at the keep, Edward Merrick had not been afforded the same luxuries more valued guests would have received.

The bed had been made, and the maid had lit a candle, in readiness for the guest's return. From what Arillion had found out about him, Edward Merrick liked the company of men, not women, and the assassin hoped that his mark returned home that night and did not stay in the bed of another.

Reportedly travelling north with three staff and two guards, in the company of others in his widening circle of society, the aspiring politician might not be alone when he returned. Arillion would have to be patient, before he struck. Surveying the room, Arillion moved to a chair, arranged before a small writing desk and mirror. Sighing, he sat down, allowing himself a soft groan. He had several hours before dawn, and he would need to be out of the city by then. He had to work fast when Merrick returned. There was much to find out in such little time, but the curiosity of it all was starting to itch, was becoming raw.

Clearing his thoughts, Arillion closed his eyes and relaxed. He would need his wits and his guile, yet again, before it was done.

Little did he know then, it would prove to be a long night.

CHAPTER FOUR

Whispers

It was deep into the night by the time Edward Merrick stumbled into his room, waving a dismissive hand towards the scowling guard who closed the door hurriedly behind his master, keen to be away from the man whose coin and favour were proving to be more hassle than their worth.

Mumbling to the drums in his head, Edward Merrick staggered towards his bed, the room spinning, the solitary candle burning his sight as he pitched towards the bed. He did not realise his fall had been stopped, was not aware, such was his state, that something was wrong, until the hand clamped over his mouth and a blade was pressed to his throat.

"Send your man away," a voice rasped in his ear, barely above a whisper, but full of warning. "Do it, now!"

Merrick nodded his head as best he could, aware that his captor was relaxing his grip, allowing him to stand on his own two feet again. Turned back towards the closed door, the steel and hand remained, guiding him forward.

"If you cry out, you die," the voice hissed again, a man's voice.

Merrick nodded, his eyes wide, his heart hammering louder than the drums of his excessive indulgences that night. What had been a day full of promise and success, was quickly turning sour on the edge of a fickle knife.

The hand released, slipping from his mouth to roughly grip his right shoulder, and the blade remained as a warning, pressed deep into the spine of his foppish waistcoat.

Finding a breath, Edward opened the door, searching for the guard who was stood dutifully to the right of his room, stifling a yawn.

"Thank you, for today," Edward blurted, wild-eyed, his words slurred. "I shall not require your services until the morrow."

The guard saluted, not trying to hide his relief, and was halfway down the hallway before his employer had closed the door.

Arillion dragged the politician back, throwing him to the bed. He locked the door and turned back, a smile slipping across his face, hidden away beneath his scarf.

The assassin observed the pathetic man before him, disliking him even more. Edward Merrick sobbed, holding up shaking hands towards his tormentor. Heavily perfumed with odour and alcohol, any expensive scent he may have worn was long-lost to a night of revelry and, judging by the vomit on his clothes, debauchery.

Arillion allowed the light of the candle to dance along his blade, before he spoke.

"Why don't you and I have a little chat about tomb robbing?" he said, stepping close.

*

Edward Merrick did not die well, and Arillion gained little satisfaction from ending the man's ambitions right there and then, other than he may have earned himself a greater fortune than he could have ever imagined that night, thanks to the politician's willing readiness to spill his guts and sell-out those he had been orchestrating the tomb robberies for.

In the end, no amount of coin promised would have saved Edward Merrick, and Arillion dragged his crescent blade across the man's throat, watching on dispassionately as the man clutched at the wound and fell back onto his death bed in a pool of spreading blood.

As the man twitched his last, Arillion moved to the candle and snuffed it out between a thumb and forefinger. Moving blindly for the door, Arillion pressed himself up against the wood, hearing nothing but the storm in his own heart, raging wildly.

He had done the Four Vales a favour this night, one its people may never truly come to appreciate. Slipping from the room, Arillion locked his success away behind him. Pushing the key under the door, back into the room, the assassin hurried away, hoping his luck held out.

If he survived the night, Arillion had just done Savinn Kassaar an even greater service, one neither of them could have ever anticipated...

Much to Arillion's annoyance, the guard who had been sleeping earlier that night, was now standing alert, snapped from his slumber, perhaps, by the return of his charges. Without slowing to draw suspicion, Arillion moved towards the man, pulling his scarf down beneath his chin before the faint torchlight revealed his features.

"A long night," Arillion observed, faking a yawn. He saw the guard nod, watched as he covered his bearded face to hide his own weariness. "You can get home now, my turn."

The man's eyes flashed brightly with hope, and then narrowed at the corners in confusion. "What's happened to Erith? I thought he was taking over from me?"

Arillion nodded. "He was, but he got called off elsewhere – there's trouble down in the city again."

Not one to pass up the chance of escape, the guard grinned. "Thanks, my friend. I don't believe we have met before."

"Tobin," Arillion lied smoothly, accepting the man's offered hand. "Enjoy what's left of your night."

The man promised he would, and Arillion waited before the guard had disappeared down the twisting staircase, before he deserted his post outside the room called the '*Greywood Suite.*'

The door to the room he had used to break into the keep previously was still, thankfully, unlocked. With his heart racing, Arillion slipped quietly into the dark room, immediately detecting the sounds of snoring from the adjacent bed chamber. Glad that he had pulled the drapes closed earlier that night, the assassin crept quietly across the lounge, stumbling over the shoes and clothes that had been cast aside hastily.

Someone coughed, but did not wake, and letting out a soft breath, Arillion hurried to the drapes and parted them. The moon was bright outside now, and flicking a wary glance behind, he could see the tangle of attire scattered about the lounge. He grinned, seeing the mix of male and female clothing, thrown about the place in a fit of hasty passion.

Certain he would not be discovered by the occupants, even if he sneezed, Arillion opened the windows and slipped out into the night.

The grounds of the estate were quiet. From his vantage point, he could tell that the Watch had been doubled now, as he could see more torches patrolling about the grounds. To his relief, the western wall was still shrouded in darkness, and pulling his scarf back up over his nose Arillion slipped deftly down the trellis and stole carefully across the pathway.

His heart was in his mouth as he made for the ramparts, and he was thankful that there were no dogs on patrol that could pick up his scent, smell the stench of death upon him.

"You there!" a voice called out from behind him, echoing away to his right. "What are you doing?"

Arillion slowed to a casual halt, but he was anything but calm as he turned about. Two torch-bearing guards were beckoning to him, from the side of the keep, and the assassin swallowed his fear, as the dark building seemingly rose up ominously behind them into the night sky.

He almost made a run for it, but Arillion knew that the alarm would be raised well before he cleared the wall. Letting out a calming breath, he made back across the misty lawn towards the two guards.

"Are you trying to lose your job?" one of the men asked incredulously. He was clean shaven, his strong face marred by pocked-marked cheeks. "You never cross the lawns, you should know that."

Arillion hung his head low in apology, hiding his cold hands under the folds of his cloak. "Sorry, it's just that it is so bloody cold tonight. I can't think straight, let alone piss it."

The man seemed satisfied by that, but the younger one with the soft beard looked past him towards the western wall. Arillion saw the confusion on his face when he saw no torches up there.

"Where–"

Arillion's crescent blade flashed from the shadows, opening up a crimson smile in the youth's throat. As the guard fell away and his torch dropped from his hand, his companion let out a roar, reaching for the sword sheathed at his hip.

Elbowing the man in his face with his left elbow, Arillion spun behind the older guard, catching him as he stumbled backwards. As the guard bellowed out a second warning, Arillion yanked his head back and sawed his knife across the man's throat, cutting off his cries for help.

Dropping the man to the lawn he had been so desperate to preserve, Arillion could hear answering shouts rise up from the east and south. Torches turned towards the sounds of commotion now, and snatching up one of the fallen brands, Arillion hurled the sputtering torch up onto a nearby balcony.

Spinning away, he raced for the western wall, bounding swiftly up the steps to the ramparts. Turning, he sent a look out across the estate, and could see that the first guard had already reached the corpses. Another roar rose up into the night sky, and away towards the main gate, the first alarm bell began to ring out across the grounds. Cursing anyone who was listening, and framed by the bright moon, Arillion was spotted by the yelling guard, who had noticed the footprints, snaking away through the mist across the lawn towards the west.

Muttering, the assassin grabbed hold of the crenulations and peered down the length of the wall into the shadows. He had taken his time climbing up the old wall earlier that night, choosing his handholds with care. This time, however, he had no such luxury, and hauling himself over the side, he held onto the wall, lowering himself as far as his frame would allow.

He heard more shouts rise up above the din of alarm, detected the first sounds of barking from the north. Drawing in a deep breath, Arillion could tell someone was racing across the grounds towards the ramparts now.

Cursing, he let out his breath and allowed himself to fall.

The city was still celebrating as the lone guard made his way through the choked streets that heaved with revellers; all dancing, singing, cheering to the sounds of fiddle and flute. On one corner, two men, with a baying crowd watching on, fought over something neither would remember in the morning. Ignoring the fray and his duty, the guard limped on, favouring his right leg as he pushed his way down the lone street known as Merchant's Walk and slipped away from the crowds down a quieter lane.

It was here that Arillion stopped – trying to filter the noise of the celebrations, trying to tell if he was still being followed. He heard nothing that gave him concern, and allowed himself a few moments to catch his wits. He had fallen awkwardly, badly twisting his left ankle as he landed. With the alarms inside the grounds of Byron Keep ringing in his ears, the shouts of pursuit chasing after him, the assassin had made his escape, hobbling down into the city to lose himself amongst the crowds.

Highwater, despite the late hour, was still celebrating, and Arillion slipped easily away from the immediate danger, blending in with the crowds, trying to avoid any militia patrols as he pretended that he had finished his shift for the night and was making his way home.

Arillion scowled. The safety of his home, wherever that was these days, seemed a long way off at the moment, and the bitter taste of his incompetence stuck in his throat – he was not used to making mistakes, and he hated the fact that he had not been able to slip away without being noticed. Furious at his perceived failure, Arillion had toyed with making his way back to Morgan Belle; to hide in The Nest for a few days – but, he knew, despite his anger, that would be a bad decision. By then, getting out of the city would be even harder – the gates watched, everyone checked as they left Highwater. If he was to escape, Arillion had to leave Highwater as soon as he could – he would have to escape the city tonight.

From his bed of rubbish and meagre possessions, a beggar watched the festivities in the street beyond, not even aware he had company. Ignoring the filthy apparition, Arillion moved away from the noise, becoming one again with the shadows and silence. The guards at the keep would be searching beyond the grounds now, in the wider city below, and as the assassin hobbled his way further down the narrow lane, he ignored the painted whore who was kneeling amongst the rubbish, her head bent low over her client's waist, as he stood moaning with his back against a ramshackle tenement building. Smiling, Arillion left them to their time together, making his way through the night towards the northern gate, the one he had entered into the city through a few days prior.

By the time Arillion reached it, he could barely walk, and he waited for some time, watching the two guards under the shadows of the gatehouse. They seemed bored, turning to each sound of merriment from within the city with wistful looks. Arillion blew into his hands to try and warm them up – it was really cold now, and as he watched on, one of the guards made his way over to a brazier to try and keep warm. On the ramparts above, Arillion could tell there were three more guards, all dark shapes against the moonlit sky, hunkered down to try and escape the cutting wind that swept down from the Great Divide.

Licking his lips, Arillion moved towards the poster he had seen pinned to a signpost and pulled it down. Ignoring the dark effigy of the masked man upon it, he rolled the parchment up tightly and made his way towards the gatehouse.

The guard who had resisted the warmth of the brazier stirred at his approach, and walked curiously forward to meet the newcomer.

"A cold one," he observed, offering a smile.

"Aye," Arillion agreed, "it is! You drew the short straw as well then?"

The guard scowled. "Yes, I did. Drew the same bloody thing last year, 'an all."

Arillion offered the man his sympathy, shaking his head. He held up the rolled parchment, so the guard could see it. "Well, I am afraid it's not going to get any better – there is trouble in the city, fighting has broken out. The Watch needs support. My captain sent me to get fresh legs."

The man frowned. "Is that how you got your limp?"

"Chasing some thief," Arillion said, nodding. "Pickpockets are preying on those who can't stand up for themselves any longer, and fighting has broken out down by the Guard Room. There should have been a curfew hours ago – shops are being looted as well."

"By the storms," the man whistled. "How many does your captain need?" He reached for the supposed orders, but Arillion distracted the man by turning away, as if he had heard a noise.

"At least three, if you can spare them," Arillion said as he looked for something, not turning back. "I have two comrades joining me shortly. They have been on duty all day and are being pulled from the chaos."

The man called for his comrade, and shouted up for two of the guards on the ramparts to join them. They muttered something in return as he explained their orders, then began to make their way down.

"Well, at least we won't be standing around in the cold," the first guard grinned, beckoning for Arillion's orders. The assassin passed them into his hand and tensed, his hands falling to his sides.

"Aren?" he barked, looking for the other guard, who peered down from the ramparts. "Stay here with our friend...?"

"Tobin," Arillion answered, sighing inwardly as the man folded the wanted poster up without reading it and put it in his pocket.

"...Tobin," the man continued. "You should have some company soon. Until then, try not to fall asleep, again."

The younger man said something untoward, and his friend laughed. "Come on!" he muttered, looking for his comrades. With a nod to Arillion, he led them off towards the city.

"Good luck!" Arillion called after them, grinning.

With a wave, the guards were swallowed up by the night, and Arillion watched them for a time. Years ago, someone had said to him that if you wanted to look inconspicuous, if you wanted to remain invisible in plain sight, carry a parchment or scroll – it made you look important, and people were more likely to trust you if you acted like you were meant to be there, knew what you were about.

Arillion called Aren down to join him at the brazier, and the young man was at his side before the assassin's hands had warmed over the flames.

"My thanks," the red-haired youth said. "I've been up there for hours."

Arillion clapped the lad on the shoulder with his left hand. As they turned back to the flames, the assassin wrapped his arm about Aren's throat and drove his knife into the base of his neck. The flames hissed from the fountain of blood, and Arillion quickly dragged the dying guard into the shadows of the gatehouse.

"Sorry son," he whispered, closing the youth's wide, staring eyes.

With a quick look back towards the city, Arillion allowed himself a thin smile. *He was free – he had made* it. It would be some time before he could risk returning to the North Vales after this night, and keen to not outstay his welcome, the assassin limped away into the night.

He was seventy-two paces from Highwater, heading up the broad path into the mountains, when the first shouts of pursuit rose up and the dogs began to bark.

Epilogue

Savinn Kassaar heard the commotion, long before the shadows lengthened and slipped under the door to his study. Placing the quill he had been writing with to one side of the unfinished letter, he threaded his hands together, propping his elbows on the ancient desk.

When the hooded figure forced his way into the candlelit room without knocking, he was not surprised, and reined in his annoyance at the intrusion as Cullen fidgeted in the corridor beyond, his face flushed red with anger.

"I tried to stop him, boss," the squat retainer began, as the assassin closed the door in his face.

"Come in, why don't you," Savinn growled, offering his guest a seat.

Arillion limped across the room and fell into the chair across from his employer. Faint light slipped underneath the door from the hall beyond, and the merchant-thief could see that Cullen's shadow lingered. He said nothing, waiting for the assassin to speak.

"It is done," Arillion said, reaching into the darkness of his cloak. He produced a folded piece of parchment and placed it on the desk between them. He tapped it meaningfully.

"What is this?" Savinn asked, cocking an eyebrow as the assassin's eyes glittered from the shadows of his hood. He had not lowered his scarf, but the merchant could sense Arillion was smiling.

"A lot more than you bargained for," came his reply. "And it has a figure of how much extra it has cost you."

The merchant's smile was more akin to the wolf behind him on the wall. "You are already getting paid a small fortune of crowns – tell me your news and I shall tell you their worth."

Arillion shook his head, waving a finger in the air between them. "That might be how you do business above the city, but down here, in the shadows, it doesn't work like that. I have here–" he paused to tap the parchment under his finger meaningfully again, "–information that everything Merrick was doing was at the behest of someone else."

Savinn's eyes narrowed. "Careful, Assassin. Your reputation serves you well, but there are limits to the depths of my gratitude... and patience."

Arillion shrugged his indifference. "My work is done for now, merchant. Merrick is dead, as you required, and the robberies, for now, should stop. You will have to decide the worth of what I have brought you, and you know where to find me when you figure it out." He rose, staring down at the merchant-thief. "You will have to be careful not to reveal your hand in this – you will need to rely on those who are your eyes and ears from now on. But when you need someone to be your hands, my swords, for the right price, are yours again."

Arillion turned away, hearing Cullen retreat back down the hallway. He crossed to the door, pausing there with one hand on the handle.

"Until next time," Arillion said, leaving the door open as he left the room.

Savinn Kassaar's mind raced and his heart was hammering as a prophetic chill stole through the room. For so long he had fought against those he knew worked against him, those that despised him enough to want his political aspirations silenced, or his throat cut.

Was one of their names on the note?

Chewing through the nerves on his lips, the merchant-thief reached for the parchment, hesitating as his hand shook over it. Sighing, he finally found his courage and unfurled it, his eyes searching for the confirmation of what he had, for some time, come to suspect.

Moments later he groaned, burying his head in his shaking hands as he realised that the fortune he owed the assassin, it seemed, was now the least of his worries.

Keen to be away to fresher air, Arillion swept down the corridor, forcing the fat wretch Cullen to get out of his way. Without a word of farewell, the assassin hurried down the steep steps towards the concealed door as quickly as his twisted ankle would allow.

It had been a wearisome, yet worthwhile few weeks for him and he ached for a brothel and a bed.

As Arillion hauled open the secret door and became one with the shadows again, he had a feeling that he would be seeing Savinn Kassaar and his coins again soon, very soon.

The end...

About the Author

Since reading The Lord of the Rings at an early age, and later, the works of his favourite authors, David Gemmell and Bernard Cornwell, Anthony has been inspired to write his own stories.

When he is not forging tales and filling blank pages, Anthony spends his time working in his local library, reading, board gaming and enjoying adventures of his own.

Anthony lives in Wales with his wife, Amy, and their cat, Mertle.

He is currently working on 'Rise of Eagles,' his fifth novel.

You can keep up-to-date with his news here: -

Website: https://anthonylavisher.com/

Twitter: @alavisher

Facebook: www.facebook.com/lavisherauthor

Printed in Great Britain
by Amazon